THE WITCH'S CHILD

By Arthur Yorinks

Illustrated by Jos. A. Smith

Abrams Books for Young Readers

New York

Library of Congress Cataloging-in-Publication Data:

Yorinks, Arthur.
The witch's child / Arthur Yorinks ; [illustrated by] Jos. A. Smith.
p. cm.
Summary: Desiring a child of her own, Rosina the witch fashions one out of
straw and scraps, but when she cannot bring the rag child to life she becomes
enraged and turns the village children into shrubs, where they stay until a kind
girl discovers the discarded doll and saves her.

ISBN 13: 978-0-8109-9349-5
ISBN 10: 0-8109-9349-X

[1. Fairy tales.] I. Smith, Joseph A. (Joseph Anthony), 1936–ill. II. Title.

PZ8.Y80Wi 2007
[E]—dc22
2006031980

Printed and bound in China
10 9 8 7 6 5 4 3 2 1

HNA ■■■■■
harry n. abrams, inc.
a subsidiary of La Martinière Groupe
115 West 18th Street
New York, NY 10011
www.hnabooks.com

For Ania, Nettie, and Elka
~A. Y.

For Claire Xiu Yi and Leo,
who have added magic to my world
~J. S.

ONCE THERE LiVED A WiTCH iN THE WOODS...

a mean, horrible witch. She was wicked and cruel and absolutely heartless, and her name was Rosina.

Rosina made it rain when there wasn't a cloud in the sky. She turned decent people to stone. She made the ground shake and lightning strike and wind roar. She was powerful and evil and had all there was to have— all but one thing. A child.

So one October night, out of bits of straw and leaves and clumps of her own hair, Rosina made herself a daughter and called her Rosalie.

But she couldn't bring Rosalie to life.

"Rise, my Rosalie," demanded Rosina. "Awake!" the witch cried out. But with all of Rosina's spells and brews, the straw girl only stared and did not say a word.

"Perhaps tomorrow," Rosina said, and she flew out into the night to rattle the resting.

The next morning, Rosina tried again to awaken the lifeless Rosalie.

"Rosalie," the witch said, "I can give you anything you want." With a wave of her hand, Rosina filled the room with toys and treats. But the straw girl only stared and did not say a word.

Rosina, in a fury, flew out her window to frighten lost souls.

Days passed, one by one, two by two, and Rosalie still did not stir. Weeks and months and seasons passed until, one spring day, Rosina noticed children playing in a nearby field. She turned and looked at her lifeless daughter and remarked, "Perhaps this will wake you, my dear Rosalie."

The witch carried Rosalie outside and, with a simple spell, lured the children to play with her. But the children did not know how to play with a girl made of straw. They twisted her and twirled her until she began to fall to pieces.

Rosina, boiling and seething with anger, made the sky turn dark and howl with thunder. The terrified children ran. But the witch raised a finger and, one by one, turned each child into a thorny bush, stunted and prickly and rooted to the ground.

"If I can't have a child, no one will!" cackled Rosina as she carried Rosalie back to her gabled house. Inside, Rosina abandoned Rosalie next to the dustbin and soon forgot her.

Thereafter, the clouds never parted in Rosina's fields, and any child luckless enough to wander in them was turned to shrubbery, knotted and stiff.

Spring melted into summer. Autumn arrived. And one late September afternoon, Lina, an inquisitive little girl, strayed too far from her parents. She missed Rosina's fields and found herself at the witch's house. She walked inside.

"Hello," Lina called out. No one was home. No one except Rosalie.

Lina looked at disheveled Rosalie and said, "Oh, poor girl, look at you. What a mess." Lina began to mend the girl of straw. She straightened her legs and stuffed her arms and brushed her hair.

"Much better," said Lina. She picked up Rosalie and hugged her and danced with her and gave her the one thing she never had—the warmth of a loving heart.

But outside a bitter wind chilled the night.
A frost was coming. And so was the witch.

Rosina flew into the house. Seeing Lina holding Rosalie, the witch raged.

"Trying to steal something, you wretch?" said Rosina. "Well, you'll do very nicely as my supper tonight, young lady!"

The witch lit a fire in the hearth and then grabbed a long knife.

"Oh, please!" Lina pleaded and burst into tears as she hid behind Rosalie. "Please, I wasn't stealing anything. Please! Someone! Help me!" Lina cried as she held onto Rosalie.

"It's too late for that, my child," said Rosina as she approached the terrified girl. But something happened.

All at once, Rosalie felt a thumping, a beating, a throbbing, a pulse.
With Lina's tears on her arms, Rosalie slowly, awkwardly wrapped those
very arms around Lina to protect her.

Rosina was stunned. In a jealous frenzy, the witch lunged forward
to grab Lina. Rosalie pulled Lina to safety as the ferocious witch sailed
straight into the fire. Being so dry and brittle and barren of love, Rosina
went up in flames, and that was that.

Rosalie held onto Lina all through that autumn night.

In the morning, Lina's parents found her safe and sound. So glad and grateful were they that they adopted Rosalie and gave her brothers and sisters and happiness and a kindly roof over her head.

With Rosina gone, her clouds departed, and finally, in the sun's embrace, the bushes that were children were children again, and their parents loved them and were thankful for them and properly cared for them, as well they should.